ANNEMIE BEREBROUCKX

presents

THE ADVENTURES OF
BERNIE AND FLORA

BERNIE

♥

FLORA

TRANSLATED BY LAURA WATKINSON

BOOK ISLAND

Bernie and Flora spend lots and lots of time together –
from early in the morning until late in the evening.

Bernie has a big garden
full of beautiful flowers and plants.
Flora's garden is only small,
so she likes to go and help Bernie out.

"What lovely flowers," Flora says. "And they smell so wonderful."
Bernie closes his eyes.
He breathes in the scent of the flowers and feels the joys
of spring tickling inside his tummy.

Bernie and Flora enjoy the same things.
They share their little secrets, and their big ones, too.
They love to talk, but being quiet together can be fun as well.

Bernie and Flora have been best friends for a long, long time.

Bernie and Flora have spent a lovely spring day together.
But now it's getting dark. It's time for Flora to go home.

"Tomorrow I'm going to surprise Bernie with a yummy breakfast,"
Flora says to herself.
"We can sit in the garden, with all the flowers.
I'm sure Bernie will love it!"

The next morning, Flora
goes shopping.
She buys a French stick, some
cheese and a bottle of milk.
And she gets some fruit
for Bernie, too.
He loves strawberries and
he always enjoys a nice glass
of orange juice.

Flora drives over to Bernie's house.
The morning sun is shining in the sky.
Flora feels very sunny, too.
She has a warm glow, deep inside.

Flora rings the doorbell and waits. But Bernie doesn't answer!
She tries again – but the door stays closed.
How strange. Perhaps he's in the garden …
Flora peers over the wall.
"Bless my beak!" she squawks in surprise.
"Someone's picked all the flowers! I wonder who it was."

Bernie's washing is hanging out to dry in the sunshine.
The plants and trees make the garden look very, very green.
But all the flowers have vanished.
The garden looks so sad.
And so does Flora.

Who would do such a thing?

Flora runs to talk to Bernie's neighbour, Annabel.
Annabel adores flowers.
"Annabel, was it you who picked
Bernie's flowers?" Flora quacks angrily.
"Of course not," Annabel says with a smile.
"I have plenty of flowers of my own.
Maybe Lou did it. He's keen on clipping."

Flora dashes to Lou's house.

Lou's garden is full of big bushes.

He's clipped them into all kinds of different shapes.

"Lou, was it you who clipped Bernie's flowers?" snaps Flora.

"Why would I do that?" asks Lou. "I don't even like flowers.

You could try asking Mo. He likes to snip."

"Mo, was it you who snipped Bernie's flowers?" Flora hisses at Mo.

Surprised, Mo looks down from his tree.

"Flowers? Me? Snip flowers?

I like to snip paper, not flowers.

Maybe Otto knows something about it.

Otto has a whole pond full of water.

And flowers need water," says Mo.

"Otto, do you know where Bernie's flowers are?" Flora squawks.
Otto laughs. "I have lots of water," he says, "but no flowers.
A pond full of floating flowers sounds lovely,
but it would make fishing very tricky."

Disappointed, Flora drives back home.
The sun has disappeared by now.
And so has that warm glow inside.

"It's so sad about all those flowers," she says with a sigh.
"Who would do such a thing? And why?
Bernie will be so unhappy.
He's very proud of his flower garden."

Flora opens the front door and ...
It's like a dream!
The living room is full of beautiful flowers.
And in the middle of all those flowers is ... her best friend.

"My dear Flora, my little flower, I love you so much!" says Bernie.
"I want to be with you, always and forever. Will you come and live with me?
And the two of us together can make a garden full of beautiful flowers."

Flora blinks.
She's so happy that she doesn't know whether to laugh or cry.
"Of course I want to live with you. I'd love to!"
Then Flora blushes.
"I thought you'd never ask."

Next spring Bernie and Flora plant
new flowers together.
They enjoy the warm sunshine.
And their garden full of flowers.
And their love for each other.
Bernie and Flora, always and forever.

Bernie

Meaning: strong or brave as a bear.

The name Bernie is short for Bernard, a combination of the old Germanic words "beran" (which means "bear") and "hard" (which means "hardy, strong"). So Bernie means "strong bear".

Flora

Meaning: flower.

Flora was the Roman goddess of flowers and spring.

Every flower has its own meaning. Bernie has so many things that he wants to say to Flora!

Acacia: You are my secret love
Anemone: My love for you will not fade
Azalea: I will take care of you
Bellflower: I am thinking of you
Carnation (red): My heart aches for you
Carnation (pink): You are always on my mind
Carnation (white): You are sweet and lovely
Clover: I promise to be yours
Dahlia: You are so elegant
Daisy: You make me so happy
Daffodil: Please love me too
Gardenia: You bring me joy
Iris: I have some good news for you
Lavender: I am devoted to you
Orchid: You are so beautiful
Peach blossom: Will you be mine?
Poppy: I dream about you
Primrose: Our love is eternal
Rose (red): You are my true love
Rose (pink): You are so graceful
Rose (white): My love for you is pure
Roses (red and white): We will be together forever
Rose (yellow): You are my best friend
Sunflower: The sun always shines when I'm with you
Tulip (red): My love for you will never die
Violet: I will be true to you

ANNEMIE BEREBROUCKX

This edition first published in 2012
by Book Island, Raumati South, New Zealand
info@bookisland.co.nz

Text and illustrations © Annemie Berebrouckx
English language translation © Laura Watkinson 2012
English language edition © Book Island 2012

Original title: Berre en Fleur
© Uitgeverij De Eenhoorn Wielsbeke 2011

A catalogue record for this book is available from the National Library of New Zealand.

Edited by Gillian Tewsley
Designed by Gert Degrande, De Witlofcompagnie, Belgium
Typeset by Vida & Luke Kelly, New Zealand
Printed by Everbest, China

ISBN: 978-0-9876696-1-2

The publication of this book has been made possible with
the financial support of the Flemish Literature Fund.

Visit www.bookisland.co.nz for more information about our books.